Across the River

An 1800s Black / Native American
Novella

Lisa Shea

D1521961

Lulu ISBN: 978-1-312-77496-4
Smashwords ISBN: 9781310471865
ASIN B00RBW12A2
D2D ISBN 9781507005392
print ISBN-13: 978-1505701265

~ 3 ~

Visit my website at LisaShea.com

Give thanks for all we have.
Say a prayer for those who came before us
and paved the way.

Across the River

Chapter 1

Tennessee, December 24, 1809

Naomi put her hand over her mouth, her stomach heaving, and she raced across the plank floor for the front door. Flinging open the latch, she stumbled out into the fresh-fallen snow, hoping to make it to the ramshackle outhouse across the clearing.

She didn't.

She collapsed to her knees, the contents of her stomach emptying across the glistening white. The sunset overhead was rich in tangerines, golds, and crimsons. Normally she would take heart in its beauty – in its sign that God's mercy still offered hope.

But not tonight.

The Blackburn Fork roiled in its wintry anger, just on the other side of a mess of brambles. The rest of the oak and maple which surrounded her small shack were barren and lifeless. The wind whistled through their stark branches as she continued to heave.

It seemed an eternity before she was done, before the last of the dried carrots and trout jerky had left her system. She picked up a handful of snow and ran it across her face, then took a fresh ball to swish around in her mouth.

A tremulous voice called from the doorway. "Mama?"

She turned, tenderness seeping into her. Johnny, her oldest child, was standing in the doorway, his dark face blending in with the shadows. He was nearly three, and already he was a handful. She could tell he would be one of those wild, willful men when he grew up.

Just like his father.

"I'm right as rain, Johnny," she assured him. "Just not feeling well, is all."

"The baby's cryin', mama."

"Go rock her. I'll be in in a moment."

His dark eyes held her, as if he might refuse out of sheer childish stubbornness - and then he turned.

Naomi sighed, braiding her long, straight, dark hair back from her face. Little Polly was almost seven months old. She was quickly becoming a toddler. She was no longer the baby of the house.

Naomi's hand went to her belly, and her throat tightened.

The child within her was.

Just the thought of that tiny life brought her both ecstatic joy and mind-numbing terror. It was the most beautiful miracle God could have given her – but could she force another child into this soul-wrenching terror of a life?

A man's voice called out from the thick woods, harsh, laced with anger.

"Naomi! You damned black injun squaw. What the hell are you doing out in the snow!"

Naomi flushed, guiltily spun, and pushed up to her feet.

Before her stood Bill Williams, the father of her children. He was a bullish beast of a man - tall, husky, with short-cropped, dirty blond hair. His skin was as white as the snow which surrounded them.

She remembered a time when his staggering strength and sharp arrogance drew her like a moth to the flame. She had been young then, barely twenty-one. She had wanted him like she had wanted nothing else on Earth. Her desire for him had blazed like the baking heat of the sun on a hot August day.

But within four brief years …

Bill's face darkened. "Naomi!"

Naomi shook herself. "I'm … I'm sorry, Bill. I got sick, is all. I must've eaten something wrong."

"Well, get back in the house, you fool. Are you fixin' to die? It's freezin' out here. You don't even have shoes on."

Naomi looked down. It was true. She was dressed just in her nightshift. The sickness had come on so sudden that she'd raced out, leaving the door wide open behind her.

She gingerly stepped through the snow back to the house, Bill tromping in behind her. She idly wondered if he'd gotten into yet another fight down at the tavern. Normally he wouldn't have been home for hours yet. But she didn't dare to ask him. She'd learned quickly not to question anything he did. His answer was often the back of his hand.

He slammed shut the door behind him, then pulled off his heavy boots. Naomi went to the fire to stir it into life. Their home was small – barely two rooms closed in by rough-hewn timber and a roof which leaked in the rainy season. The room they were in held a rough-hewn table, four wooden chairs, and two open shelves filled with their meager possessions. The other room held the large bed for the adults, a smaller mat for Johnny, and the crib for young Polly.

Soon they would need another.

Bile rose in Naomi's throat. She staggered to sit in the chair nearest her.

Bill snapped a look at her. "What is with you, woman? You best not be slacking off 'cause I wasn't around. You see me?"

She pulled a smile onto her face. "I'm fine. Really. Everything will be set for Christmas tomorrow."

She bit her lip. She shouldn't ask. She really shouldn't ask. But the thought of young Johnny in the other room, and his fervent pleas, made her continue. "Were you able to get that toy horse that Johnny wanted?"

Bill turned with the bottle of whiskey in one hand, a metal cup in another. His eyes flared. "What are we – *in the pines*? Made of money? Of course I didn't buy the spoiled brat that horse. Twenty-five cents! I could buy a quart of rum with that!"

Naomi glanced over. A pair of large eyes were peering from the corner of the bedroom.

She stood, putting herself between Bill and her young son. A note of pleading came into her voice. "Please, Bill. It's Christmas. And Johnny's been so good –"

Bill's brows came together. Deep creases shadowed his face.

For a heart-stopping moment Naomi could see clearly why the locals all called him "Devil" Bill.

Her throat tightened, and she put her hands up before her. "You're right. Of course. Absolutely

right. I'll find him something else for a present for
Johnny."

Bill's glower shimmered with heat. "You're
damn right you will. No son of mine is gonna to
grow up spoiled. He's gotta work for what he gets.
That's how a man lives. He takes what he wants
and he don't let no meddlin' crow-black woman
tell him otherwise." He coughed and spit into the
corner. His voice dropped into a grumble. "Damn
crow women's all alike."

Naomi glanced behind her. The round eyes
were gone.

She looked to Bill. "I gotta check on the
baby." Her hand went automatically to her
stomach, and she flinched.

Bill's eyes lit up in a leer. "My seed take
a'hold again so quick? I done waited the three
months before I mounted you. My mammy always
said three months is what she needed to gain
strength for the next one. Kept her from dying in
childbirth, like all those weak women do. But you
can't keep a man off forever." His grin grew.
"Ain't healthy for a man to go too long without."

Naomi's hand tensed against her belly. He
couldn't know. Not when her soul was already
twisted with worry.

She shook her head. "I'm not pregnant," she
insisted. "I'm just sick."

He looked her over, then spat again. "Sick," he growled.

She half-thought he would come at her, to force his way past her feeble resistance and use her as he always did. It seemed a lifetime ago that his touch brought pleasure. Now she just prayed for him to be brief.

His eyes glowered …

At last he slugged back his whiskey and turned to pull his boots on.

She took a tremulous step forward. "Are you going out again? But Bill, it's Christmas Eve."

He turned, glaring at her. "That's right. And I'm a-gonna go celebrate."

He pulled open the door, stepped through, and yanked it shut behind him.

Hollowness settled on the house. Naomi wrapped her arms around herself, trembling. With effort, she drew herself together. She had two young children who relied on her for protection.

Her hand slipped to her belly.

Three.

She looked again at the door, at where the Devil Bill Williams had left her. Undoubtedly he was trudging the three miles into town to seek out a woman who craved his fiery heat. Once, long ago, Naomi had been that woman. The one whose heart pounded with anticipation when she heard his heavy footstep. She had taken great pride that he had chosen her – out of all the women in this wild part of Tennessee – to be his.

Now she knew better. Now she prayed for the day that she and her children could escape – to somehow, against all odds, be safely free.

There was a movement at the bedroom door. Johnny's dark eyes were on her again, bright and large. "Mama, Polly's hungry."

"Of course, sweetie. You're such a good boy to help your little sister like that. Come on, let me tell you both a story."

His gaze lit up. "A story? After bedtime? But Papa will be mad."

She stood and moved to take his hand. It seemed so small and delicate within her own.

She smiled down at him.

"It'll be our little secret. Okay?"

He nodded, his eyes intent.

She moved into the relative darkness of the bedroom, the only light coming from a flickering candle in a tin canister. It sat on the lone dresser at the foot of the bed. She moved to the rough-wood crib. Polly lay there, a dark raisin against the tumble of brown blankets, her dense, curly hair tight against her tiny head. Naomi lifted out Polly and brought her to a breast. Polly latched on hungrily, settling down to suck, one hand gently resting on the curved skin.

Naomi sat on the bed, leaning back against the lumpy pillow. She pulled the quilted blanket up, and in a moment Johnny had wriggled his way in against her. He nudged her in her side. "The story!"

"Yes, yes, the story," she reassured him. "Just give us all a moment to get settled in."

Polly contently sucked away, and Naomi shifted to account for the weight of both of her children. At last she found the sweet spot between the lumpy mattress's edges and sighed with contentment.

The candle flickered, sending spots of light across the ceiling.

Naomi looked down at her son. "Ready?"

He nodded, his eyes pinned on hers with eager anticipation.

She smiled fondly. "All right, then. Let's begin. Tonight is Christmas Eve …"

The horse toy for Johnny sprung to mind, and she flushed. She would have to make something new for him once he went to sleep. She had no idea how she would do it, but she'd find a way.

She could see similar thoughts going through his young mind, but he stayed quiet, his eyes shining with trust. He seemed to be sure that somehow his mother would make Christmas all right.

His trust in her staggered her.

She found strength growing in her voice. "It's Christmas Eve. Many, many years ago, and far, far away, there was a quiet town called Bethlehem. It was very cold out that night, and all the taverns and inns were full. But a pair of visitors came into the town. Joseph and his wife, Mary. They needed a place to stay, but they were very poor, like us, and Mary was pregnant."

Naomi's hand slipped to her own belly.

Johnny's brow scrunched. "But Mama, we're not poor. We have a big house!"

Naomi drew him in close, pressing a tender kiss against his forehead. "You are right, little one. We have so much to be grateful for."

Polly squiggled, and Naomi moved her to the other breast.

Johnny yawned. "And then the mama and papa went into the barn with the chickens and the sheep and the goats. That way they could be warm and dry."

Naomi smiled at her son. "You know the story well."

"And then the baby Jesus was born, in the straw. And that's why we go to church tomorrow."

"That's exactly right, my darling. We go to celebrate his life. He taught us to be kind to others. To care for each other."

Polly had settled down now to just gently mouthing Naomi's nipple, half-asleep.

Johnny gave another yawn, this one larger. His voice was a mumble. "Mama, do you know what I want for Christmas?"

Naomi closed her eyes. Her young son deserved so much in life. So much. And she would do her best to see that he got it.

Her voice was tight when she spoke. "What, my love?"

He draped his tiny arm across her waist. "I want Daddy not to be mad any more."

She drew him in against her, tears welling in her eyes.

"I know, sweetie. Now, go to sleep. Santa will be visiting us soon, and I'm sure he'll bring you something nice."

Johnny nodded his curly head, and then his breath eased into an even rhythm.

Naomi looked down at her two sleeping children, then her hand went to her belly.

Strength crept into her spine. Whatever it took, she would make a better life for them.

Chapter 2

Naomi carefully tucked Johnny's arms into his jacket, then buttoned him up tight. His hat and scarf were the last two items to bundle him against the cold. His gaze did not turn from the small blue cloth horse he clung to tightly with both hands. He turned it over and over in his hands, marveling at its silky, black mane and its button eyes.

Naomi gave Johnny's dark, curly head a fond tousle as she sleepily yawned. It had taken her all night, but she'd manage to cut enough fabric from the bottom of her favorite blue dress to fashion the cloth horse and create the toy for her son. The summer dress would be shorter, certainly, but by the time it was warm enough to wear it again she was sure she'd be able to buy fresh fabric to add to its length. All that mattered today was the joy in her young son's eyes.

A rough cough came from the bedroom, followed by a snarl. "Naomi! You crow Lumbee squaw! Where the hell are you?"

She winced, then walked quietly to the doorway of the bedroom. "It's Christmas," she reminded Bill. "I'm taking the children to church."

"Damn preachers," he grumbled, pulling the blanket over his head. "They're licken' to bleed you dry, is all."

"I'll be back by lunchtime," she promised.

"You'd better. And don't let me catch you talking to those negroes, either. They's born *across the river*. We're better than them, and don't you forget it."

She pressed her lips together, then went back to her two young children. She drew Polly up in one arm, took Johnny's hand in her other, and stepped out.

The world was beautiful. It was decked in a stunning white frock, laced with sparkles, and the sky overhead was high and brilliant blue. The Blackburn Fork bubbled and burbled over its rocks, and a blue jay called out from a nearby pine.

Johnny looked up at her while they made their way along the deer path through the dense woods. "Mama, why does Daddy hate negroes?"

Naomi reflexively put a hand to her own face. Her father had been from Ireland, gathered up by the English for slavery, along with many other children from his village. And her mother's father had been Irish as well. But her mother's mother had been dark skinned, dark eyed, some sort of mix of negro and Indian. Her granny didn't even know her blood for sure – she'd been raised a servant and had never known her true parents. All she could do is guess by the chocolate-brown skin and long, straight, glistening hair.

Naomi took after her.

When Naomi had been young, it hadn't mattered much. She and her four older siblings had played, laughed, and taken it for granted that people came in all shapes, sizes, and colors. They had black friends and red friends, brown friends and pink friends. The country was not even twenty years old when she was born. Everyone was in the same rough-shod fix. Everyone pulled together to make it work.

But times were changing. With every passing year she could see the lines forming. The English were being separated out, treated differently - elevated. The rest – Indian, black, Irish – were becoming second-class citizens.

She wondered where it would lead.

Johnny pulled her hand. "Mama?"

"I'm sorry, sweetie, what did you ask?"

"Mama, does daddy hate me because my skin is dark like yours and not white like his?"

Naomi dropped to her knee, pulling her son close. "Oh, Johnny, of course not. He loves you and your sister dearly. He just doesn't like to show it much."

"But daddy said darkies – crows - were slow and weak."

She tousled his curly hair. "Daddy just gets grumpy sometimes, sweetie. My brother, William, looks like us – and so does his wife, Elizabeth. Do they seem slow and weak to you?"

Johnny shook his head. "No, Mama. Uncle William is strong. When he helped us, that time the roof fell in, he got the whole thing fixed in less than a day. And Aunt Elizabeth made us that yummy dinner afterwards."

Naomi tweaked his nose. "You little sow cat! I think you had eight helpings of her sweetnins that night."

Johnny blushed, but she could almost see his mouth water at the memory.

Naomi smiled, standing again. Just like her own family, Elizabeth's Oxendine line was made up of mutts. A swirling mix of Lumbee, black, and who knew what else. Elizabeth had skin several shades darker than their own, not having been watered down by the Irish.

Naomi's brother adored Elizabeth, and Naomi felt blessed that the couple lived just an hour's walk away.

She patted Johnny's cheek. "Your cousin, Hiram, will be at church, so we best get a move on."

Johnny nodded, his eyes shining. "Hiram's just like me – he's brown like the tilled earth."

Polly wriggled against her, and Naomi adjusted the carry strap. "That's right, Johnny. The Good Lord made every person with their own color. We are like snowflakes. We're all different, and God wants us like that. It doesn't matter if my skin is dark or your daddy's skin is light. All that matters is how we use the gifts we have."

She folded her son's young hand within her own, snugged her daughter up on her chest, and together they stepped along the snowy path. Clumps of briars lined the edges, their brambles standing out sharply against the white. Off in the distance Naomi could hear the soft shush-shush of the river wending and twisting along the rocks.

It was another half hour before they approached the small settlement tucked around the church. The homes here were sturdier than her own, some with a second floor or attached barn. The church was painted white and boasted an elegant steeple up above its large double doors. Pastor Smith, his creased, brown face showing his advanced age, was standing in the doorway, shaking hands. He smiled as Naomi approached.

"Naomi! There you are. Always a pleasure to have you and your adorable children in our flock. Come on in – the fire's stoked and your pew is all ready. William and his family are already here."

Naomi nodded to him, then moved inside. Sure enough, she could see her brother's sturdy form, his curly, dark hair starting to streak with grey. Alongside him was his willowy, dark wife, Elizabeth. Elizabeth glowed with serenity and contentment; her dark-blue dress fit her with well-tailored style. At her side was their son, Hiram. Hiram was just two years older than Johnny.

Johnny's eyes lit up with delight. "Hiram!" He raced forward to sit alongside his cousin, and immediately their heads were together, sharing whatever it was young boys found most fascinating.

William and Elizabeth smiled fondly at Naomi as she settled onto the smooth wood of the pew. Their voices came in harmony. "Merry Christmas, Naomi."

Her heart warmed as she looked up her older brother. He'd been born a full ten years ahead of her, and he'd always kept an eye out for her. She could remember countless times that he'd pulled her down from a too-high tree or carried her on his strong shoulders when her tiny legs had given out.

William's gaze held her with tenderness, and then he looked down at the cloth horse in Johnny's hands. His face eased into a frown. "I thought –"

She cut him off with a shake of her head. "Johnny likes his horse. Santa brought it for him." She smiled at her precious son. "Don't you like your gift, my sweetheart?"

Johnny nodded enthusiastically. "He's gonna ride me wherever I want to go!"

William gave a tight smile to his nephew, his dark face creased with tender worry. "Of course you will, Johnny. You can do anything you set your mind to."

Elizabeth looked over at Naomi, her plump, glowing face the color of rich coffee. "Are you feeling all right, Naomi? You look plum peaked."

Naomi twined her fingers against the pew, willing herself not to reach for her belly. "I'm fine," she assured them. "Just a long night, is all."

Elizabeth's eyes held concern. "Why don't you three come over after the service, to have Christmas dinner with us. There's always plenty of space."

She paused, then her voice added warmth. "David will be there."

Naomi barely remembered Elizabeth's brother. He had been at the wedding, of course, some ten long years ago. Naomi had been perhaps fourteen at the time, and she had been swept up in the beautiful dresses, the rich music, and the wealth of delicious food. She had barely taken in the cacophony of strangers who had attended.

"Bill wouldn't like it," she found herself saying. "He wants us to come right home."

William's brow creased. "Naomi, Bill shouldn't be keeping you from your family. Not on this day, of all days. Family is what Christmas is all about."

She blushed, her immediate reaction being to shield Bill. It seemed that was what she spent half of her life doing.

"Bill *is* our family," she insisted. "We should be with him."

William glanced at Elizabeth, and something passed between their gazes. Naomi's heart echoed with hollowness. She wished with all her might that she had that kind of a connection, that kind of a warmth with a man.

Despair sunk deep within her soul, and she turned her gaze to the humble altar before her. Pastor Smith's church was simple, but it was tended to with great love. The beams were square and solid. The wood was polished until it glowed. The cross hanging on the back wall had been carved by William just last year, and the near-perfect roses curling around its joints were heartwarmingly beautiful. They always seemed to speak to Naomi about the fragile beauty of life; about the powerful nature of sacrifice.

Jesus had sacrificed his life so that his children might life.

She, every day, did the same.

She fought back the tears, and her hands clenched even harder on the pew back before her. If only it weren't so hard. If only there were a man out there who would care for her children the way they deserved – who would provide an environment where they could flourish and grow.

Where they would feel loved.

Where she would feel loved.

She closed her eyes and prayed.

Time drifted … passed … flowed like the Blackburn Fork as it headed south, south, to vanish into the midst of the vast wilderness.

She relinquished herself. She placed herself in the palm of God.

She let go.

There was a voice behind her, rich and resonant. It soothed her, wrapped around her soul, and made her whole.

"Merry Christmas, everyone."

Naomi opened her eyes and turned.

He had to be David. He had Elizabeth's rich color, one of coffee and dark chocolate. His well-chiseled face was framed with rich, brown curls, and his eyes were amber and deep. He wore a neatly-cared-for wool coat over dark brown shirt and trousers. But it was the eyes that held Naomi. Eyes that echoed with strength, purpose, and a sense of steadfast loyalty.

Her stomach fluttered, and she could barely breathe.

David's gaze moved fondly from William to his sister, then down to his two young nephews. Finally his eyes drew to hers. They widened and held.

She could easily get lost in those eyes. Wholly, eternally lost.

He seemed to come back to himself with a shake. "You must be Naomi, William's youngest sister. I remember, now. You danced at their wedding. You shone. I'd never seen anyone so happy."

Naomi's world fell away. She remembered it clearly. The way the music thrilled her – the way she spun with joyful pleasure. It seemed a lifetime ago. And now every day was a struggle to simply survive …

David's brow creased. "Is everything all right?"

She dragged her gaze away from those insightful eyes and looked down at her weathered hands. Her throat was tight. "I'm fine," she croaked out. "It is good to see you again, David. Merry Christmas."

He took the seat next to her. She could feel the warmth radiating off of him. Somehow he had a bearing of strength about him – that no matter what kind of blizzard, flood, or plague of locusts might sweep down, that he'd be there to stand against it.

Elizabeth's soft voice eased in to her roiling thoughts. "David is here visiting us for the holidays. He'd been down in South Carolina with our father, keeping an eye on him."

David gave a gentle smile. "Well, our father raised all eight of us no matter what it took. Harsh, frigid winters or broiling hot summers, he found a way to make it work. So it seems only fair for us to care for him now that he's getting on in age."

William nodded. "Our father only had the five kids, but he was good to us. I know, when he was finally freed of his servitude, that he counted every day a blessing. He swore none of his children should ever have to endure that."

William looked over to David. "Your father, Cudworth, talks about his own release day every time Elizabeth and I visit. How the day of his release was one of the greatest days in his life. Because it meant he could finally court your mother – and have all of you."

Naomi held Polly close to her chest. The sleeping child made a soft mewing noise before settling in again. Naomi closed her eyes. Both of their families had been through so much. Both fathers had endured harsh service to cruel masters and had to wait the length of a contract to finally be free. Whatever she endured now, she knew she should be forever grateful that she was a free woman.

Pastor Smith carefully made his way down the aisle to the front of the small room, and the group settled down into silence. He looked out over his congregation, his rheumy eyes seeming to touch on each person in turn.

"Let us pray."

Pastor Smith's service always soothed Naomi. He gave just the right amount of encouragement and advice. His sermons were a mixture of readings and reminiscing. He conveyed the news of the land in terms she could understand. She'd never learned to read or write, and in this quiet backwater of Tennessee there weren't many passers-by. Pastor Smith used his network of contacts to keep the locals informed of the changes that were going on.

As he finished with the main sermon, he drew his hands together. "My friends, I have some sad news. Meriwether Lewis, who was part of that famous expedition to explore this great land of ours from 1804 to 1806, has perished just a few hundred miles west of us, at the Natchez Trace. It appears he might have been murdered."

Naomi's shoulders pulled together, and she drew Polly in tighter against her. Those roads were rife with robbers and cutthroats. The world they lived in was a dangerous one. It reminded her – again – of why, despite everything, she stayed with Bill. He had a foul temper, and a quick hand, but he would defend his home like a rabid wolf defended its cave.

She could not imagine any thief getting past him to hurt her or the children.

William spoke up. "Pastor, do they know who is responsible for Lewis's death?"

The pastor shook his head. "Seems they shot him and slit his throat, then made off with all his funds. He was heading into D. C. to talk with the President." He sighed. "The man goes all the way to the far ends of our great land, on a Holy quest, and with God's blessing he survives. Then he simply tries to transverse Tennessee and our own boys take him down."

He looked across his flock. "It's been six short years since we acquired from Emperor Napoleon the lands to our west – Louisiana, Missouri, and the like – and doubled our territory in one fell swoop. Louis and Clark were instrumental in helping to explore this new territory and determine is boundaries. We have much to be grateful for, to this man."

His mouth turned down. "But news has come from France that Napoleon is preparing to divorce his beloved Josephine, all because she cannot produce an heir for him. He will instead seek out a woman who is fertile. We should pray for him … and for her."

The congregation's heads bowed as one.

Naomi's hand went to her belly. To think that Josephine would give anything she possessed to be able to create a new life. And here Naomi was, tortured by her state.

David's voice came in her ear. "Naomi, are you all right? You're as white as a haint."

Naomi drew Polly in against her. "I just need some air." She looked over at Elizabeth. "Could you watch Johnny for me?"

"Of course," assured Elizabeth. "Johnny and Hiram will be fine."

David took her arm, and together they walked up the aisle to the main doors. She slipped through them, stepping out into the brightness of the afternoon. The sharp tension slid away as she took a long, deep breath of the cool air.

A soft snow was falling, light, fluffy, adding a glistening sheen to the wintry scene. There were a scattering of simple homes along the dirt road. Pastor Smith's two-story home was right alongside the church, the split-rail fence neatly set. She could almost see the wealth of wildflowers which would sprawl along that length in the warmth of summer.

Then there was the trading post, a rail for tying up horses out front, large windows showing neat shelves of nails, flour, and cloth. That was where Johnny had laid eyes on the shiny tin horse.

She drew Polly in closer.

David stood alongside her, his breath coming in long, even draws. His voice was low and quiet. "I've been talking with my sister. That devil Bill decided he had better uses for Johnny's Christmas money, didn't he."

Naomi flushed, pressed her lips together, her eyes welling. Bill could do whatever he wished to her, but Johnny was only a child. A sweet, innocent child who deserved all that life had to offer.

David's eyes strayed to the two-story house at the far end of the street. "Come over for dinner after the service, Naomi. Get some solid food into you and the kids. Elizabeth's serving a chicken, and we've got sweet potatoes, too. And chess pie."

Naomi's mouth watered. It'd been a long while since they'd had fresh meat. Bill seemed as if he could live on whiskey and water. Perhaps even just whiskey.

It took every ounce of energy she possessed for her to shake her head. "I can't. Bill's expecting us home right after the service."

"Christmas is about family," he murmured. "You should come and be with your brother. Let the cousins play together."

Her throat was tight. "Bill is my family."

"And yet he refuses to marry you. Even after you have lived together for years." His voice dropped. "Even after you have borne two children for him."

She winced. She wondered just what kinds of conversations David had been having, while visiting her brother. Again, she found herself rising to defend Bill, to justify his actions that, in her own heart, tore her to pieces.

"Bill's an independent man. He don't take much stock in the church. But he's been there for me and the kids."

David's voice gained a growl. "Been there like he was for you last night?"

She flushed hard, drawing Polly in close against her. Her throat went tight. "What do you know about last night?"

David's dark face was lost in the shadows. "I know I saw him down by Sally's, skulking around like a dog after a gyp in heat."

Naomi turned her head away, her chest constricting. It was one thing to know Bill was unfaithful to her. It was another to have him parading it around for all the village to see.

David's voice reached her from a distance. "Naomi, you deserve better than this. You deserve someone to love you. To care for your children. To give you all the life you deserve."

Polly's tiny eyes creased open, and her delicate, dark face scrunched in consternation. She began making soft, mewling noises.

Naomi moved to sit on the bench alongside the church. She pulled her coat over to shield her daughter, and then adjusted her neckline to give her child access to a breast. Polly eagerly latched on and began drinking.

David's eyes shadowed. "Naomi, you can't shield your children forever. What happens when they grow older – when they understand more what is going on in their life? You're barely clinging on as it is."

He paused, and his voice lowered. "What happens if you get pregnant again?"

Naomi wrapped her arms around Polly, holding her close. Darkness closed in on her, threatening to overwhelm her.

She looked up into David's eyes, those warm eyes which held the promise of security. She'd only been talking with him for ten minutes and already it seemed she'd known him a lifetime.

Her throat grew tight.

"David, I —"

There was movement behind them, and the doors opened. Villagers streamed out, offering warm wishes; beaming with smiles and laughter. At last Pastor Smith emerged, his arms around Elizabeth and William's shoulders, the two boys scampering out before them. The Pastor was glowing with pleasure. "Absolutely. I would love to come spend the afternoon with y'all." He looked over at Naomi. "Shall you be joining us?"

Johnny bounced over with a smile. "Oh, can we, can we, Mama? Hiram has a new toy rifle he wants to show me! His daddy made it for him. It's carved and everything!"

Naomi looked up into David's eyes. She could see the unspoken thoughts resonating in them.

It took her every ounce of strength to look away, to shake her head. "Johnny, your daddy's waiting at home for us. We should go back."

His small face fell. "But Mama, daddy will just be angry anyway. And Aunt Elizabeth is cooking chicken! Real, fresh chicken!"

Naomi's mouth watered at the thought. She resolutely pushed herself to standing, settling Polly in against her more securely. She put her other hand out to her young son. "Come now, Johnny. It's time to go. Say goodbye to everyone."

Johnny's face darkened, and he almost looked as if he would willfully refuse. But at last his small shoulders sagged and he wrapped his fingers into hers. He looked around at the people standing around him. His voice sounded more like a dirge than a holiday greeting. "Merry Christmas."

A chorus of echoes responded, and Naomi turned to begin the long, cold trudge back to her small, desolate home.

Chapter 3

Bill spun on her as she walked in the door. His voice was rough with anger. "Where the hell have you been, you lazy negro? I'm starving!"

Naomi flushed. "I'm so sorry, Bill. I'll get started on dinner right away." She hurried past him into the bedroom, tucking Polly into her crib. She then turned to press a kiss on Johnny's forehead. "You play in here with your sister," she murmured.

Johnny's eyes were wiser than his young years. He solemnly nodded. "Yes, Mama." He sat on his mat and looked down at the cloth horse in his hands.

Naomi hurried back into the main room. She dug into the rough box by the shelves, bringing out a pair of misshapen potatoes. She drew the knife from the pocket at her hip and deftly sliced them up into small, neat chunks.

From another box she carefully selected a slim sliver of dried fish. Then she went to the fireplace to place all of her main ingredients into a large cast-iron pot. She added in a handful of dried sage and a dusting of salt. Then she stepped out the doorway to the drift of snow leaning against the house. She made a hollow in her skirt and filled it with a pile of snow.

When she was set, she lumbered with the snow-filled skirt back inside and carefully emptied the snow into the pot. A few minutes of stoking the flame, and the meal began its course.

Bill wrinkled his nose, drinking down another slug of his whiskey. "Potato stew? Again? God, woman, can't you cook anything else?"

Naomi kept her gaze on the pot. She knew better than to rise to Bill's arguments. "I'm sorry, Bill."

His voice echoed hers with sharp mimic. "I'm sorry, I'm sorry." It gained an edge. "That's all I hear from you. How you're sorry about this. Sorry about that."

"I'm –"

His face darkened, and Naomi bit off the automatic apology. She focused on stirring the meal. Its aroma wafted through the room, and her stomach rumbled.

Time passed. Bill's rough hand moved his mug of whiskey from the table to his mouth. There were the quiet sounds of Johnny playing in the bedroom. Naomi's sole attention was on the meal before her. She willed it into life.

Bill twisted in his chair, and the legs squeaked against the wood floor. "C'mon, I'm hungry."

She stirred through the liquid, watching as the spices swirled in the broth. "It's not quite done yet."

His brow drew together. "Woman, I said I'm hungry."

She flushed, but went for the wooden bowl. She carefully ladled out a portion.

His frown deepened. "C'mon, that's barely a sip."

She dropped her eyes, any response carefully dampened by years of training. She attentively scooped another ladle-more of the soup out of the pot. There would be just enough left for Johnny. She brought the bowl over to Bill, laying it in front of him. She turned to bring a spoon down from one of the shelves.

He grabbed it out of her hand, then scooped steadily at the broth before him. He grunted while he ate.

Naomi went back to the pot and carefully stirred at the stew, watching the potato slowly infuse the liquid with its flavors. Her stomach twisted with hunger, but she fought it down.

A pair of eyes peered out from the bedroom.

She smiled gently at him. "Come on out, Johnny. Your dinner's ready."

He scampered out to his chair, sliding into it without a word. When she brought over his bowl, he dug into it with enthusiastic energy.

Shadows stretched across the room, and Naomi went to the large, pillar candle on the mantle, lighting it carefully from the fire.

Bill stood, his eyes drawing down Naomi. "C'mon, Naomi. Time for you to give me my Christmas present."

Naomi flushed, but she patted Johnny on his arm. "I'll be back soon, honey."

Bill's eyes shone. "Not too soon."

* * *

Naomi carefully eased herself from beneath Bill's snoring form. Darkness had settled in earnest, and she felt her way across the room to the main living area.

She found Johnny curled up, asleep, by the embers of the fire. She stroked her hand along his curls, then picked up the poker to stir the glowing coals.

Her stomach growled, and she laid a hand over it, willing it into silence. She settled down against the wall, brought her knees up against her, and wrapped her arms around them. She looked around the small room, at the rough-hewn walls and the thick fabric hanging over the windows.

The tears came slowly at first, and then flowed like a waterfall. How had things come to this?

She still remembered clearly the first time she laid eyes on Bill. She'd been staying with her brother, helping him and Elizabeth with young Hiram. Holding that tiny infant in her arms, her whole body sung with the desire for a child of her own. Then, when she'd finally gotten Hiram to fall asleep, she'd stepped out into the dense, August air, as thick as molasses. Her soul had radiated with unquenchable desire.

In that moment, the Devil Bill Williams had come sauntering down the road, a bull looking to take over a new pasture.

His golden skin had shone in the baking summer heat. His carved face glistened with sweat; his natural-colored cotton shirt bulged out along his rippling muscles. There was something in his eyes – a sense that nothing could stand between him and something he wanted.

His gaze had come to her – and stopped. His eyes boldly, slowly traced down her form, soaking her in.

She'd flushed. Nobody had ever looked at her in that way before.

Then his eyes firmed with ambition. He'd stepped forward …

Naomi shook herself, coming back to the present, coiling herself more tightly. He had seemed like everything she wanted. Strong. Powerful. Able to take care of himself. William and Elizabeth had warned her to take it slow – he was a drifter – but Naomi hadn't listened. She had plunged in, head-first, sure that her desire for him could see them through anything.

Now she wasn't so sure.

Finally her tears slowed and she wiped her face with the sleeve of her dress. She moved to her young son's side, curled up around his body, and drew him in tight.

Chapter 4

Naomi stood by the river, holding Polly against her chest, watching as her son chunked stones across the roiling surface. He managed to get one to bounce and he threw his arms into the air in victory.

"Did you see that, Mama? Did you see?"

"Yes, that was amazing!"

He beamed, then grabbed at another rock. "I can get it further!" His brow screwed in concentration and he set at it.

A birch tree to her right shimmered, and then a wren hopped out onto a nearby branch, its small tail bobbing in rhythm.

She looked at it, her eyes welling. "Oh, look, Johnny. It's a wren. It's here for wren day."

Johnny spun in a circle. "Wren day! Wren day!"

"Your grandpa always loved wren day," she smiled down at him. "He grew up in Ireland. There, the day after Christmas was a special holiday."

"For wrens!"

"Yes, for wrens," she agreed. "The boys would catch a wren and then go around town asking everyone to donate money in order to bury it. Then they'd all have a big dance in the evening, to celebrate."

Johnny smiled up at her. "I like to dance."

"And you're a very good dancer," she agreed. "Your uncle William used to dance with me every wren day. My father would play the fiddle, my eldest sister, Mary, would sing, and we'd dance all night long."

"We should have a dance!"

Naomi glanced back toward the house, hidden through the trees. "I don't know, sweetie. Bill really doesn't like to dance."

Johnny's face fell.

Her heart went out to the small child before her. The wren on the branch hopped closer, and it seemed a sign.

"I'll see what I can do."

He brightened, and he nodded. He seemed to believe she could work miracles.

Somehow, she would.

She brought out the fishing gear, got herself set, and after an hour of chilly, attentive work she had hooked a plump pumpkin seed. Her stomach turned inside out in hunger but she held it in, bringing her prize home. She held it out to Bill as she stepped into the room. "Look what I've got you for Wren Day, Bill! I'll grill it up, just the way you like it."

His eyes lit with interest. "Now that's the way I should be eating," he agreed. "Even if it is for that stupid Mick holiday."

Johnny looked up in confusion. "Grandpa's name is William. Just like Uncle William."

Bill's eyes sharpened. "Mick means he's Irish, you dolt. He was born over in Crack-filth."

Naomi pressed her lips together. "Carrickfergus."

Bill laughed. "Right. And he was dirt poor. The bottom of the bottom." He turned to his son. "So you know what happened?"

Johnny shook his head.

"Well, boy, the English moved in with a giant broom and swept up all the dirt. They gathered up all those louse-ridden kids and packed them into ships. Sent them over to the colonies to be good little slaves."

Johnny looked up at Naomi. "Grandpa was a slave?"

"Many were slaves," agreed Naomi sadly. "But your grandpa was lucky. He was an indentured servant, so he gained his freedom once he turned eighteen."

Bill snorted. "He was definitely lucky. Micks are worse than Negros. You could buy six Micks for the price of one Negro, and if a few died off, you'd still have a few left over."

Johnny's eyes grew wide.

Naomi held the sunfish up. "I should get this ready for you, Bill – I bet you're hungry!"

Bill's eyes fixed on the fish. "Johnny, stop bothering your ma. She's busy."

Johnny dropped his eyes. "Yes, Papa."

Naomi followed her son into the bedroom, then laid his sister down in the crib. She gave her son a kiss, then whispered in his ear, "I'll save you a piece. Don't worry."

His eyes lit up, and he smiled at her.

Naomi returned to the main room and carefully gutted and prepped the fish. Then she stoked up the fire, getting it ready, before kneeling down before it. She attentively grilled the fish until it was crisping on the edges while maintaining that delicate moistness within.

She glanced behind her. Bill had his back to her, pouring a mug full of whiskey.

She bent down, breaking off a corner of the fish and laying it on a stone. Then she turned with the remaining meal. She moved to a plate, sliding the fish off and layering it into pieces.

He smiled in pleasure, breathing in the aroma. "Now this is more like it." He went into action, breaking down the fish, shoveling the pieces into his mouth as quickly as he could. It was only a few minutes before a sprawl of slender bones remained.

He wiped his mouth off on his sleeve, then drank down the rest of his whiskey. He turned to the bottle. He frowned as he held up the empty container.

He drew to his feet. "I'm going to the tavern for the night." The corner of his mouth quirked up into a sharp grin. "Wren day, after all. Need to celebrate."

Naomi held her breath. If she seemed too eager, he might not go. "Are you sure? We could always stay home together and –"

He gave a coughing bark. "Are you deaf, crow woman? I said I'm out of whiskey. I'm not sitting around this house without some liquor to get me through the night."

"Of course," she demurred. "I'm sorry."

He barked a laugh, then burped. He crossed the room and drew on his coat. When he was set, he turned to look toward the bedroom. His brow creased. "Hey, pappy sack. You be good while I'm gone!"

Johnny came to the door of the bedroom. He somberly nodded. "Yes, Papa."

Bill swept his eyes to pin Naomi for a moment, as if to warn her, too, to behave. Then he stepped out into the fading light.

Naomi moved to the door, watching until he disappeared in the far elms. Then she shut the door and moved to the fireplace. She carefully gathered up the remaining piece of fish, calling out, "Johnny!"

He was in his chair in a flash, and she laid down the plate before him with a warm smile. Then she gathered up Polly and sat down alongside him, feeling her daughter as her son joyfully ate the fish meal.

When he had finished with his dinner, she cleaned up the table. She glanced nervously at the door, but she knew that Bill would be gone until early in the morning.

She gathered up Johnny next to her. "Would you like to go see Auntie Elizabeth and do some dancing?"

He eagerly nodded.

She bundled him into his jacket, carefully tucking in the scarf around his slender neck. Next she drew on her own, thin coat. She took one last look around, then stepped out into the darkened night.

The moon shone high overhead, and she took Johnny's hand with a smile, walking the well-known path toward the village. She began humming, and after a moment the words sang out.

"The wren, the wren, the king of all birds,

St. Stephen's Day was caught in the furze,
Although he was little his honor was great,
Jump up me lads and give him a treat."

Johnny laughed in delight. "Jump up me lads!
Jump up me lads!"

She tousled his head. "That's right, lambkin."

"But what's a furrs?"

"Furze," she corrected. "Your grandpa says
it's an evergreen bush. Sort of like a pine tree, but
short and fluffy. It's where little birds like wrens
would live in Ireland."

His eyes glowed. "Oh! A bird bush!"

"Exactly. So the boys would go out to catch a
wren, on St. Stephen's Day, which is today. And
then they'd go door to door asking for money to
bury it. The chorus goes:

"Up with the kettle and down with the pan,
And give us a penny to bury the wren."

Johnny swung his arms with delight. "Up with
the kettle! Down with the pan!" He turned to his
mother. "Mama, why don't we have a kettle?"

"We don't need one," she explained. "We just
heat water in our pot, and it does as well. Means
there's fewer pots to clean."

He skipped along at her side, his feet making small, round holes in the soft snow. "So what's the next verse?"

She grinned at him.

"As I was going to Killenaule,
I met a wren upon the wall.
I took me stick and knocked him down,
And brought him in to Carrick Town."

"Where's Carrick Town?"

Naomi shrugged. "It's somewhere in the middle of Ireland. I don't really know."

"But you said grandpa came from CarrickFarrus."

"Carrickfergus," she corrected. "That's over on the eastern coast, near England. It's part of why the English could sweep up my father and all his young friends so easily. The soldiers just went up and down the coast gathering up the poor boys and girls."

Johnny frowned. "Why didn't the parents stop them?"

Naomi gave his hand a squeeze. "I'm sure they fought back, but sometimes there's only so much you can do, if the other person is stronger."

Johnny looked up at her with big eyes. "Like you and Papa?"

Her shoulders tensed, and it was a long moment before she nodded. "Like me and Papa."

There was a motion in the shadows up ahead, and she froze. There were robbers throughout Tennessee, and, heck, throughout the entire young country. But she'd never had anything of value to worry about them stealing it.

Until now.

She pressed Polly close to her breast and drew Johnny behind her. The snow glistened in the moonlight, shimmering silver dripping from the fir trees along her side.

Naomi's throat was tight. "Come out. Show yourself."

A moment passed … then two … then David stepped from the dark shadows.

She flushed. When she'd met Bill it had been like a tornado hit her. She was swirling, spinning, unsure of her footing and relishing the wild abandon. But when David looked at her, it was deeper, richer, like the sturdiness of the mountains draped in the gentle softness of a morning mist. His gaze was the deep amber of a sunset, and his eyes held hers as if they'd never let her go.

His voice was low with concern. "You shouldn't be out here all alone."

She released her tight clutch on Johnny's hand with a relieved chuckle. "I know. But Bill's off at the tavern again, and Johnny here wanted to dance. In honor of the wren, and all. So I thought we'd come by my brother's house and have some music."

David nodded, falling in at her side as they continued ahead. "I'm sure they'd like that a lot. They're worried about you, you know."

Johnny looked up with big eyes. "Worried about Mama? Why?"

David glanced at Naomi, and his brow creased. "Well, for one thing, she's looking a bit thin."

Naomi's hand automatically moved to her belly. She strove to keep her face even. "I'm … I'm not feeling well, is all."

Johnny nodded enthusiastically. "She got sick all over the snow yesterday. She was out there for *hours*."

David's eyes shadowed. "Naomi, are you all right?"

"I'm fine," she reassured him. "I'm sure I'm over that cold – or whatever it was."

"When's the last time you ate?" he prodded.

Johnny beamed with pride. "Momma caught us a fine pumpkin seed! Daddy ate most of it, but she saved me the best piece of all."

David patted his head. "I'm sure she did. She is a good Mama, isn't she."

Johnny glowed. "She's the best in the world."

Naomi's foot caught on a root hidden in the snow, and she tumbled. David's arm swept up around her, sure and firm, bringing her back to her feet. The warmth of him soaked through her, and for a long moment she leaned against him.

Suddenly she remembered seeing David at the wedding. As everyone gathered for the ceremony, Elizabeth had been nervous, almost trembling, in a beautiful dark-blue dress with spring flowers in her hair. The bride-to-be had walked toward the church, stumbled - and David had been right there at her side to be her support. He had seemed so mature and adult, even though Naomi knew now that he was only four years her senior. He had stayed right at Elizabeth's side, soothing her, lending her his strength.

Naomi had thought how lucky Elizabeth was, to have a brother like that, and to be marrying William, who Naomi loved dearly. She wondered if, when it came time for her to marry, if she would be as fortunate.

And then she'd met Bill …

Naomi wrapped her arms around herself, shivering.

David looked down in concern. "Are you all right?"

She nodded. "I'll be fine. Really."

He nudged his head. "Well, we're almost there. We'll get some hot cider into you, some fresh stew, and I'm sure you'll feel better."

Johnny perked up. "Do you think Aunt Elizabeth will have pecan pie?"

David smiled. "I'm absolutely sure she'll have pecan pie for you."

They rounded the corner, and the village was laid out before them in ivory splendor. Warmth eased through Naomi's heart. It was just the way it should be. Snow traced along the roofs and danced along the edges of the windows. Wagon tracks wore down the path along the center of the road. Elizabeth's home shone with golden light.

Johnny set out at a run, streaming for the house, and Naomi reached out a hand to draw him back.

David patted her reassuringly on the arm. "Let him go. He won't get far."

The gentleness of his hand soothed her, and she drew Polly in closer against her. For a moment, for a brief, shimmering moment, they were almost like her dream of a family. She had children she adored. A man worthy of them stood by her side.

If only it could be true.

Johnny hammered on the front door of the neatly-kept home, and in a moment it was drawn open to laughter and smiles. Hiram tumbled out to draw him into a warm hug. Above him, Elizabeth looked from Johnny out to the street and her grin grew. "Naomi! I'm so glad you could come out! Ready to celebrate St. Stephen's Day with us? You know it was one of your father's favorite holidays."

Naomi nodded, and when Elizabeth put her arms out for Polly, Naomi handed her young daughter over with a smile. David was at her back, helping her with her coat, and it was almost as it should be. One big, happy family, content, relaxing in each other's company.

Elizabeth and William's home was beautifully kept, with polished wood floors and dark blue curtains on the windows. A fire flickered merrily in the fireplace, and a pot of fragrant stew hung over it, setting Naomi's stomach to rumbling. A trio of wooden chairs were pulled up around the fire, and further back was a long wooden table with a bench on either side. A pair of candles at its center flickered with a gentle, welcoming light.

To the left a set of stairs headed up, and Naomi knew that the two bedrooms upstairs gave a privacy to the adults that she could only dream of.

It was an Eden.

Elizabeth turned in place, cuddling the young girl in her arms. "Ah, Naomi, I wish I'd been able to meet your father. He sounds like an amazing man. He must have had all sorts of great stories to tell, of the things he went through."

"He died when I was only ten, so I wasn't able to hear many of them," Naomi murmured. "I remember him swinging me up onto his tall shoulders and running around the yard. I remember him singing songs in a rich, Irish brogue. I would fall asleep to those songs. It soothed my heart."

William walked into the room, smiling at his sister. "He loved our mother dearly," he stated. "And she, him. They used to sing together every night. And when special holidays came around, like Christmas or St. Stephen's Day, it just gave them even more reasons to enjoy life."

Johnny lit up. "Wren's Day!"

William grinned. He tousled his nephew's hair. "*La Fheile Stiofan*, as your grandpa would say."

Elizabeth took Naomi by the arm. "Why don't we sit down and have a snack, and the boys can do a Wren Day parade for us."

Johnny and Hiram erupted into cheers of delight, but Naomi could barely hear them over the loud gurgling of her stomach. It seemed weeks since she'd eaten properly. She settled down at the table, willing herself to be patient while Elizabeth tucked Polly into a basket, fetched a pottery bowl from the shelf, and moved to the large, cast-iron pot.

Opposite her, William reached up to the top of the shelf and drew down a fiddle, bow, and bodhran. He handed the bodhran over to David, then settled onto one of the chairs by the fire with the fiddle. He plucked experimentally at the strings, tuning it, then looked over at David.

David stood by the fire, his eyes caught on Naomi's.

Naomi soaked him in. She felt … safe.

Elizabeth moved between them, breaking the spell, and placed the fragrant stew down before Naomi. Naomi took up the spoon and tasted the first mouthful.

She groaned with pleasure.

It was *amazing*.

David's face eased, and he nodded. Then he began thumping out an intricate rhythm with the bodhran.

William tapped his toe in time, and then he wove his melody in with it. The words flowed out, heavy with an Irish accent, as he sang the song the way he'd learned it from his Irish father.

"The wren, the wren, the king of all birds,
St. Stephen's Day was caught in the furze,
Although he was little his honor was great,
Jump up me lads and give him a treat."

Johnny was in his element now. "Jump up! Jump up!"

Hiram echoed him in delight. "Jump! Jump!"

The two boys leapt and whirled around the living room, laughing in glee.

The song frolicked along.

"Up with the kettle and down with the pan,
And give us a penny to bury the wren."

Johnny and Hiram made hand motions as they went up and down, round and round.

Naomi hummed along with the music. She would have loved to sing, but this food was just too good. Her stomach was demanding she give it more … more … more …

"As I was going to Killenaule,
I met a wren upon the wall.
I took me stick and knocked him down,
And brought him in to Carrick Town."

The boys enthusiastically whacked away at imaginary wrens. Naomi wondered if she should feel sorry for the ghostly birds, but at the moment she couldn't bring herself to care. Little Polly was safely nestled in her basket, snoring away. Johnny was having more fun than he'd had in months.

And she was getting full … she was getting full …

> "Droolin, Droolin, where's your nest?
> 'Tis in the bush that I love best
> In the tree, the holly tree,
> Where all the boys do follow me."

Johnny seemed to love that word. "Droolin! Droolin! Droolin!"

Hiram laughed. "Da, why was the wren drooling?"

William chucked at his son. "The word's *droolin*, and that's Gaelic for wren. Your grandfather would call them droolins all the time."

Hiram seemed to like this explanation, for he joined in with Johnny, swirling around, yelling out, "Droolin! Droolin! Droolin!"

William winked at David, and they kicked the song into a higher gear.

> "We followed the wren three miles or more,
> Three miles or more, three miles or more.
> We followed the wren three miles or more,
> At six o'clock in the morning."

Hiram and Johnny took each other's hands and spun around in circles, like a small brown whirlwind. Naomi sat back in contentment,

watching them, and then took a long drink on her
warm cider. It was rich with fragrant spices.

Elizabeth smiled over at her. "There's more
stew, you know."

Naomi shook her head. "I am full, really. That
was wonderful, as always."

William played a lively bridge on the fiddle,
and then they plowed into the final verse.

"I have a little box under me arm,
Under me arm, under me arm.
I have a little box under me arm,
A penny or tuppence would do it no harm."

The boys raced in circles waving their arms
about them. "A penny! A penny! A penny!"

Naomi tapped her fingers on the table in time
with the music, a smile glowing on her face.

Elizabeth watched her for a moment, then
stood and went over her brother. She took the
bodhran from David, deftly maintaining the beat.
She nudged her head over to Naomi.

David held Naomi's gaze, then moved to
stand above her. He put out a hand.

She looked at it for a long, powerful moment.
Just one dance. It couldn't hurt to have a tiny
token of fun. To pretend, for a little while, that her
world was full of laughter. Of family.

Of love.

She slipped her fingers into his.

The world shimmered away. Her brother's fiddle soared, the rich melody of a freed robin. Elizabeth's voice twined in harmony. The children's laughter filled in the crevices, making it just right.

Naomi's world reformed fresh and new. She was back home again, her mother's rich voice soaring, the fiddle playing, the drumbeat rolling. The boys swirled around her, laughing, cheering.

David moved with her, perfectly in time, his body meant for hers.

Naomi held back the tears. If only it had been David walking along the road, that fateful day. If only it had been David's eyes she had caught; David's world she had been drawn into.

If only it had been David she had ended up with.

How different her life could have been. She wouldn't spend every night crying herself to sleep. She wouldn't spend every morning praying for some way – any way – to get her children away to safety.

David's body turned with hers, spiraling, and she was lost.

The music drew to a rousing finale, and the room filled with cheers and laughter. Then David was gazing down at her, his eyes rich with concern, twined with emotions she found it hard to name.

His voice was rough when he spoke. "Naomi, what is it?"

She opened her mouth to speak.

The front door slammed open, rebounding against the far wall with a crash. A massive shape staggered into the room, bear-like, glowing with fury. Calloused hands clenched into fists, and Bill's eyes shone red with the heat of a thousand fires.

"What the hell is going on here?"

Chapter 5

Naomi was split into two equally powerful desires. One was to cling to cling to David – to hope he could shield her from the hellfire which was about to descend. The other was to leap away from him, to strive to prove to the Devil Bill that this was all some wild, innocent, catastrophic mistake which would never, ever happen again.

Then Bill stepped toward her son, and the choice was clear.

She sprang into motion, swooping up Johnny and pulling him close. The words flowed out of her mouth like the river rushing high in the spring, pushing aside all in its tumultuous path.

"It's St. Stephen's Day, Bill! Don't you remember? So we were celebrating with the wren song. It's a tradition, for my family. Just a silly tradition. And that's what families do, right? They carry along their traditions, with the brothers and sisters. So I was just here with my brother William, and sister Elizabeth, and brother David, and we were singing the wren song for the boys!"

Johnny nodded energetically. "The wren song!" he chortled. "Droolin! Droolin!"

Bill's glower deepened. "Who the hell is droolin'?"

Naomi pulled her son even tighter against her chest. "Droolin's just the Irish word for wren, Bill. It's how the song goes."

Bill spat on the floor. "Damn Paddys. Worse than negroes. 'Least negroes have some sense of respect. They know their place. But the damn Paddys get uppity. Think they can be real people. Like the rest of us."

Hiram ran to his father's side, wrapping his thin arms around his father's leg.

William's face stayed calm, but there was a line of tension in his shoulders. "Bill, I'll ask you to speak respectful in my home. Both of my parents were Irish."

Bill snorted. "Yah, your father was raw Mick, snatched up by the English for a slave and sold to the highest bidder. But your Ma, I heard about her. Sure, her father might'a been Irish. But seems that ma of hers was some different stock."

He reached forward to grab hard at Naomi's arm. She bit in the cry of pain as he wrenched it and held it toward the ceiling, so her thin dress sleeve slid down, revealing the dark skin beneath.

He gave a hard laugh. "Straight, dark hair, like an Injun's. But dark skin more like dirt brown than red clay. So she ain't even a full breed nothin'. She ain't even a half-breed Mick. She's some sort of a mongrel mutt. The kind you kick 'neath the stairs when it gets in your way."

David's face went still. "That's the mother of your children you're talking about."

Bill's face burnished with flame. "Damn right it is, and don't you forget it. She's my property now. I'm the one who popped her, and I'm the one who owns her." His voice took on a sneer. "So all you *family* can stay away, because she's got her own family now. And we do things diff'rent. My way."

He looked down at Naomi. "Get the brat. We're going home."

He gave her a push, and she stumbled before she regained her feet. Her face flushed with shame. It was one thing for him to treat her like this in private. That she could take. But for him to disrespect her in front of her family – it was almost more than she could bear.

She scrambled over to Polly, drawing the sleeping infant up in her arms. Then she scurried through the silence of the room to her coat, sticking the arms through the holes one at a time. She spoke apologetically over her shoulder to Elizabeth. "I'm sorry, I should have just stayed home. I didn't mean to cause any trouble."

Elizabeth's fingers were twined together, and she looked between her husband and her brother. "Oh, Naomi –"

Bill reached out toward Johnny, and Naomi quickly stepped between them. "I've got Johnny," she assured Bill. "C'mon, maybe I can catch another pumpkin seed for you. I bet you're hungry after your evening out."

"Damn right, I'm hungry," he growled. "Got into a fight with Richard Carter and damn near broke three of my fingers." He gave a snorting laugh. "Better than Richard, though. His nose's broken in two places. Will take him months to breathe right again."

Naomi drew Johnny close. Richard had three sturdy brothers, and she had no doubt that they'd be seeking revenge for their younger brother's injuries. If they were all caught on the open road …

She bundled Johnny into his coat and then stepped through the open doorway. "C'mon. The sooner we get home, the sooner I can catch that pumpkin seed for you."

Bill flexed his fingers, and Naomi tensed in near-panic. He half looked like he wanted to make some sort of a point – to do something to further prove to the watching family that he was master of Naomi and the two children. But then he twitched

as his bruised fingers brushed each other, and he
growled. He spat again on the floor and nodded.

"Get in motion, woman."

Naomi risked a look back. Elizabeth and
William were looking at her with sorrow and
concern. Hiram was clinging to his father, his face
buried against his father's leg. And David ...

Her breath caught.

There was a fire in his gaze, a fierce flame,
and she knew, from the very depths of her heart,
that he would attempt the impossible.

He would try to set her free.

Her soul glowed with bright terror laced with
scrabbling hope. It could get him killed. It could
get them all killed.

But there was the tiniest, most desperate
chance that he might actually wrench them loose.

She clung to that hope with all her heart.

Bill growled, and she spun, drawing along her
son and daughter. Together they stepped through
the door.

The moon had slid higher in the sky, and the
light shining down seemed cold, almost harsh in
the way it created sharp angles and deep shadows.

The deeper they walked into the woods, the
more Naomi's trepidation grew. A curving birch
created the black shadowed ripple of a snake,
slithering toward them, set on attack. The
shimmer of branches in the wind was the creeping

movement of a coyote. The crisscross of elm was
a cage holding back a wild beast – but the large
opening to the left showed where he had escaped,
and he was stalking … stalking …

There was a noise behind them.

Naomi's heart leapt into her mouth. Not here.
David could not confront Bill here. Not so soon.
Not in front of the children. Not when Bill was
drunk and riled and fresh from a fight.

Bill would kill him.

She had no doubt in her mind. Bill was a
brutal, cold, unstoppable force of nature. And then
David would be gone, and she would be lost .. lost
…

Bill turned with a growl. "What the hell is it
now?"

Three large, burly men stepped into the
clearing, their breath frosting in their air before
them.

The Carter brothers.

Chapter 6

Naomi pulled Johnny behind her, shielding him with her body. She wrapped her coat tightly around young Polly, hiding her from view. Then she glanced nervously at Bill. Surely he would at least think about backing down with these kinds of odds?

One look in his small, pig-like eyes and she knew her answer.

Never.

The largest of the three brothers, Jim, stepped forward. He was a mirror image of the other two – dark skin, dense curls, and a face which spoke to a parentage of negro, Lumbee Indian, and Portuguese. His hands clenched into fists. "You done went too far, Bill. Our brother's in bad shape. Seems as if you drove something into his brain."

Bill's smile was wide. "Serves the bastard right. You know what he called Sally? Called her a whore, he did. He had it coming to him."

Jim's brother, Sam, stepped up alongside his kin. "That's 'cause Sally *is* a whore. I was with her, myself, last night."

Bill's growl shook through Naomi's soul, and she froze in place, unable to think. Maybe if she just remained still – stock still – he would forget she existed. Forget she, and her two innocent children, had ever entered his life. And then they could be safe.

Bill's voice grated through the crisp air. "*I* was with Sally last night," he snarled. "You're a liar."

Sam's eyes shone with satisfaction, and he gave a gap-toothed grin. "That's 'cause you done came after me. You were getting her sloppy seconds. And when you were pumping yourself into that whore, you were pumping into –"

Bill's primal scream of rage echoed off the distant mountains, and Naomi dropped to her knees, drawing Johnny in hard against her. The world would end. It would rise in fire, and ash, and Bill the Devil would preside over its destruction, his eyes flashing lightning.

Then Bill dove into the fray.

Naomi held Johnny's head against her coat, shielding him from the scene. Her own eyes were clenched tight. But she could hear the sounds. The sickening crunches. The ground-shaking thuds.

The sharp groans of a man injured. The brutal snap of a bone. The rattling …

Hours passed in a raging inferno.

Slowly … staggering … silence descended.

She carefully, slowly, opened her eyes.

Sam was sprawled on the ground, his face coated with blood, his eyes glazed. One of his legs was bent at an unnatural angle. The third brother, Todd, was crouched over him, trying to shake him into coherency. Jim was looking down at Bill's prone body, a sturdy branch in one hand. By the looks of Bill's body, the stick had landed quite a number of times already. He was covered with welts. Half of him was blood-stained, and the other half would be purple by morning.

Naomi shuddered. If she'd thought his temper was bad normally, the coming weeks would be Hell incarnate. A very real fear entered her that she and her children might not survive.

Then Jim turned slowly to look at her, the stick still in his hand. His gaze slid down her form, following her curves, then back up again. A hot leer lit his face.

The bottom dropped out of Naomi's world.

She drew to her feet and took a shaking step backward, pulling her children with her. "Please, we'll just go. We'll just go and we didn't see nothing. Nothing at all. Please let us go."

Jim's breath was coming in long draws, and his eyes were pinned on her. "Bill always kept you for himself, he did. Kept that luscious form of yours locked away. But Bill's not able to stop us now. And it would serve him right if we were to take our spoils from our fight."

Todd stood, his eyes shining with desire. "Yeah, our spoils," he agreed. "Take her back to the house. Show her what real lovin' is like."

Naomi's voice was tight. "Please! The children! You can't –"

Jim raised his stick. "I can do what the hell I please. Don't you be ordering me around!"

Johnny's voice rose at her side. "Mama?"

Jim stepped forward. "You shut that kid up, or I swear –"

Naomi spun, grabbing up Johnny's hand. "Run!" She sprinted hard back the way they'd come, toward the village.

Thundering came from behind them, and Naomi swept up her son, her legs pounding faster than she ever knew they could. If only they could make it to the clearing. If only someone could hear –

A hand grabbed the back of her trailing coat, and she screamed, tumbling. Johnny and Polly rolled into the soft snow, and Polly began hollering at the top of her lungs.

Naomi flung herself forward, but Jim was hauling her back by her coat, and she couldn't untangle herself.

Her voice burst out in garbled panic. "Take Polly! Run! Run!"

Johnny hesitated a moment, torn, and then he grabbed up his younger sister, turned, and fled into the darkness.

Todd came up, huffing, staring into the shadows. "Want I should go after them?"

"Nah, they're like homing pigeons. They'll just run on back to their aunt's," stated Jim, drawing Naomi up.

She backed away from him – and slammed into the sturdy form of Todd behind her.

Jim chuckled, reached forward, and ran his hand possessively down her breast.

She shuddered.

Her voice choked out of her. "Please, just let me go. I promise I won't say a word. I won't make one sound about what happened here."

He squeezed her breast, his eyes darkening with desire. "Oh, you'll make a sound, all right. Bet ya don't with Bill. We'll get you goin' again. We'll just see what that Devil has to say about that."

His hand moved to latch solidly around her wrist, and the other still held the thick branch. She knew that one swing of that would knock her out flat.

But her children were out there, alone, fleeing into the dark, snowy night.

She waited … waited … and then spun, twisting, wrenching her arm clear of his grasp. She turned to flee –

Wham.

Chapter 7

Naomi blinked into awareness. She was being carried over a sturdy man's shoulder. The snowy world beneath her swayed to and fro with the man's gait. Her ribs ached where she was slumped over his frame. She was shivering with cold – her coat must have been abandoned somewhere back in that clearing.

A man was on either side.

The Carter brothers.

Tears welled in her eyes. Every ounce of her prayed that Johnny and Polly had made it back safely to the village. Nothing else mattered. These men could do what they wanted to her. They could kill her. But her young children were innocent in all of this. She knew Elizabeth and William would take good care of them.

Tears dripped down her face. Maybe the children would be safer with their aunt and uncle. Certainly, they'd be far better off than if Bill tried to raise them on his own.

God, anything but that …

The men slowed, and a small glimmer of hope rose within her. Maybe they had changed their mind. Maybe they were going to bring her back to Bill. The thought of facing his wrath filled her with tight fear, but somehow she would do it. She knew he would blame her for everything; would say it was her fault he was out in that woods to be ambushed and taken down. And he would make her pay.

But she would face it all, if these men would just –

They turned, and she saw the house.

It was a crude, one-story hovel, tucked in against a small hill. A run-down outhouse was on the far side of it. In the distance she could hear the Blackburn Fork tumbling and cascading along its rocky path.

Not another soul was in sight.

She found her voice. "Please, just let me go. I need to get to my children."

Jim gave a barking laugh. "They'll be with their new family by now. You, you got a new purpose. You gonna be our Sally."

Todd laughed at that. "Yeah, *our Sally*."

Jim stepped to the door and kicked it open. There was just one large room within. A rough-hewn table had two benches, one on either side. The fire glowed with soft embers, and four chairs were in a rough circle near it. On the other wall were four dirty mats piled with dingy blankets.

Richard's scrawny form was curled on one, a thick wadding of shirt pressed to his blood-crusted face. He turned with a groan. "What the hell?"

Jim grinned. "Hey, there, Richard. We done taught Bill a lesson he won't ever forget. And we brought us a little ree-ward, too. Lookee here."

Richard twisted and pushed himself up to sitting. His hollow eyes took in Naomi, first in confusion, then in growing heat. A leer stretched across his face. "That might even make my fight worth it," he muttered, "if'n I get a piece of that."

Jim laughed. "Oh, you'll get more than a piece, brother. You'll get every part of her. After what ya been through, I think I might even give you second dibs."

Richard's eyes creased. "Second?"

Jim gave Naomi a shake. "I done carried her the whole way," he shot out. "I earned the break-in. Lessen' you gonna fight me for her?"

Richard put up his hands. "Second's fine with me. Just as long as I get my time."

Jim's eyes shone. "Oh, we'll have plenty o' time. Don't ya worry 'bout that. Bill's gonna be out for a long, long while."

Icy fear plunged through Naomi's core. The one time she could have used Bill's fury – the one time his massive strength and quick fists could have finally served her some good – and he was not there to save her.

She was on her own.

Jim spit on the floor, then lugged Naomi over toward the mats. He called over his shoulder, "Sam, you stir that fire up. It'll be a long night. And Todd, you get the whiskey. We gonna have ourselves a party."

Naomi scrambled in panic, but Jim had a solid hold around her waist. As he neared the mat he gave her a hard flip. She went flying through the air, slammed onto the ground, and her breath blew out of her. She struggled to draw in a fresh one. Then a solid weight landed on her chest, and she choked. Jim had straddled her, his face hot with desire.

His voice was rough. "You are a pretty one, aren't you. No wonder that Bill is always keepin' you at home. Wants you all for hisself, he does." He ran a hand down her cheek. " 'Bout time he shared."

Naomi shivered, trying to wriggle free. But Jim's body held her pinned securely to the mat. She drew in a deep breath to scream, and she nearly gagged on the rancid stench coming from the blanket beneath her.

Jim laughed. "Scream all you want, missy. We're out in the wilds here. Like it that way, we do. Private. Quiet. Ain't nobody to hear you yell for miles." He leaned forward, his breath fetid. "And I like it when my woman hollers. I like a woman with fire in her."

Naomi's cheeks were wet with tears. "Please," she pleaded, her body shaking from exhaustion and fear. "Just let me go. I'll do anything. Please."

Todd waved a bottle of whiskey in front of Jim, and Jim grinned. He put the mouth between his lips and tipped it back. The amber liquid slid down the glass in a long, glugging swallow.

He wiped his lips on his sleeve, then handed the bottle back to his brother. "That's better." His eyes lit up with hot desire. "Now watch and learn, little brother. You'll see how a woman should be ridden."

Naomi was sobbing. She didn't care. She was far beyond caring. "Let me go. Just let me go."

Jim put his hands at her neckline, side by side. "Nah. I think we'll see what's beneath this dress of yours. I've always wanted to know."

He turned to look to his brothers with a grin. "Well, boys, it's Christmas!"

The men burst out in cheers.

Jim pulled.

Wham.

The door flew open, slammed off the side wall, and rebounded hard. Two men strode in to the room, their chests heaving as if they'd just finished a race for their lives. Their eyes swiveled, searched –

And solidified with grim determination.

Chapter 8

Naomi stared between William and David it utter shock. They could not be here. Not in this room. Not with the four Carter brothers turning, grinning, solidifying into a wall, and forming a permanent barrier between her and her saviors. Not when that mass of blackguard muscle bunched and rippled, intent on one thing.

Destruction.

William's eyes swept the younger brothers before coming to rest on Jim. His voice was cold and steady. "You let her go. Else you and your brothers will be facing far more than a broken nose."

Jim laughed, flexing his fingers. "Got a sweet spot for your little sis, do you? Always thought you might. You seemed a little too fond of the girl. A little too attentive. Shoulda known you were keeping her on the side. Though that's just plain greedy, if you ask me. That wife of yours is a purty piece. Mighty purty."

He glanced at his brothers. "I says we go have a visit with her, once we put these two men down. Bring her back to join her sister-in-law."

Todd eagerly nodded. "Yeah, two of them. Less sharin'. More action."

David's stance was low, steady, as if the strongest hurricane could not knock him off his feet. His voice was guttural. "You won't be touching either woman. Ever."

Jim grinned. "When we're done with you, I think we'll tie you to the table. So's you can watch, all night long, and see how it's done proper."

Naomi pressed herself up against the back wall, drawing her knees to her chest. Her heart pounded against her breast, trying desperately to escape. It was four against two. She had to go for help. But help was miles away, and it would all be over by the time she returned.

Richard's hand slid to his back hip, and she saw the gleam of metal.

Panic rose within her. She called out, "Knife!"

David dodged left, throwing up an arm, and the knife slid along his forearm, gouging a red streak.

Jim bellowed in victory, and the Carters drove in hard.

Naomi curled herself into a tight ball, unable to move or breathe. Jim slammed a beefy fist down toward William's crown, and William slid it, taking the blow on his upper back. He spun with a right hook, rocking Jim back, causing him to stagger back onto one knee. William swept with his leg, snapping Jim's knee out from beneath him and cascading him onto his side.

Todd slammed a fist into William's kidney, and William coughed out a shuddering groan.

Sam and David were trading punches faster than Naomi could follow – jab, block, jab, uppercut. Richard launched a kick at David's knee, but he spun his body to take the blow on his upper thigh. Sam's next punch landed hard on David's chin, rocking his head back, and David stood for a moment, stunned.

Todd launched himself at William's back, clinging onto him like a possum baby on its mother. William clawed at the arms around his neck, struggling to pull free the grip that constricted ever more tightly. Jim grinned, rising to his feet, launching a kick at William's groin.

William turned, blocking it. Then he dropped to one knee, flipping his shoulders forward and vaulting Todd off of him into the fireplace.

Todd sprawled into the blaze, his thin clothing catching like tinder. He screamed in agony, whirling, a firestorm come to life. He raced out through the open door and into the dark night.

One down.

Sam crept toward David, trailing his injured leg. David's eyes took that in with bright attention, and when he spun his next kick, he aimed his boot square for that kneecap. Sam screamed in agony, falling to the ground, clutching at his leg.

Naomi's breath thundered out of her. They might do it. They might just actually survive.

Jim rushed at William, driving him back, slamming his body into the wall by the door. The entire shack shuddered with the impact. Jim drew back a beefy fist, launching it toward William's head. William dodged at the last minute, and Jim's fist rammed hard into the sturdy wood. His scream of pain nearly shattered Naomi's ears.

Richard looked around at his fallen brother, then his eyes lit up. He dove for his brother's hip, coming up with a six-inch-long hunting knife. His eyes gleamed with satisfaction as he turned on David. "Gonna gut you like a doe," he grinned. "Gut you stem to stern."

David circled him, his eyes fully attentive, his breath coming in even draws.

Naomi looked around frantically for something – anything – which could help. Her eyes latched on a food-caked cast-iron skillet which was propped up by the table. She slowly, carefully crept her way over to it. The men were all wholly focused on their opponents – she might have been a field mouse for all they paid attention.

Her hand closed around its cold handle.

Richard's back was to her, his greasy hair hanging in strings, and his knife hand came up high. His voice was bright with eager delight. "Gonna gut you!"

He dove forward.

Naomi launched, swung with all her might, and drove the skillet down as hard as she could onto his skull.

Richard dropped like a stone.

Jim let loose a room-shaking bellow, then he drove at William, his hands at William's neck, holding him against the wall with his massive bulk.

David threw himself on Jim, wrapping a muscular forearm around Jim's neck. He locked it in place with his other. And squeezed.

Jim constricted his fingers … pressed … he coughed and suddenly released William, his hands scrabbling for his own neck. William collapsed to his knees, drawing in deep breaths, his own hands going to his throat.

David stepped back with Jim, pressing, easing him to his knees. Jim's clawing at his throat slowed, feebled, and finally he hung limp in David's arms.

David gave him one more moment for good measure, and then released the body to fall on the floor. It lay there, inert.

William and David knelt still for a moment, their breath coming in long heaves, their eyes sweeping the three prone men around them. And then both gazes drew to where Naomi stood, still clutching her cast iron skillet.

Naomi glowed. They had come for her. They had stood against all odds and kept her safe. It was a miracle. A true miracle.

David pressed himself to his feet, his eyes wholly on hers. His voice was rough.

"Naomi –"

There was a staggering motion in the doorway, and David spun, putting his body between the newcomer and Naomi.

Naomi raised her skillet high. If Todd was coming back for more, despite his burns, then they would be ready for him.

The man stepped into the firelight, his pale skin shining like a haint, his fiery eyes glowing with the damned depths of hell.

Bill's voice shook with fury. "What the hell have you done to my woman?"

Chapter 9

Bill looked as if he had crawled out of the depths of Hell itself. His torn clothing was soaked with blood. One eye was purpling, half-shut, and his face was mottled with bruises. But the fierce glower in his face showed he had no intention of backing down.

His gaze went more attentively to Naomi, and red heat flared in his face. "Jesus Christ, Naomi!"

Naomi looked down – and stopped. She'd completely forgotten that Jim had ripped open her dress just before her two saviors had arrived. Her front was peeled open, and her breasts hung fully revealed in the crisp night air.

She dropped the skillet with a clatter and clutched desperately at the pieces of her dress. She frantically drew the ragged edges in, seeking to soothe Bill's mounting fury.

David spun, drawing his own blood-spattered shirt off with one easy motion. He strode over to stand behind Naomi, then eased the warm fabric down over her head. He carefully, gently ran his hand along her neck, drawing out her long hair to lay it on her back.

Time stopped.

Deep ease soaked into Naomi's bones.

She could feel the warmth of his garment cocooning her, wrapping around her. It echoed the warmth of the man just behind her. If she took one step backward, she would be pressed against his strong chest. She would be safe, so safe, and nothing could hurt her again.

She eased her arms through the holes …

Bill stormed across the small room, grabbing her by the wrist and turning her. "What the hell happened, Naomi?" His eyes flared as he looked down her body. "Did you let them *touch* you?"

David's eyes glowed with heat, and she stepped between them. She couldn't let Bill hurt the two men. Not when they had risked their lives to save her.

"I'm fine, really I am," she assured Bill, her gaze shining with desperation. "The Carters didn't touch me at all. They meant to, but then William and David stormed in –"

"They shoulda waited for me," Bill snapped. "Shoulda let me do it. They robbed me of my chance." He turned to glare down at Jim's senseless body, then kicked him hard in the ribs. Jim didn't make a sound.

Bill's voice dropped into a low mutter. "Hardly any fun, now." He kicked again.

William's growl came from the far side of the room. "We should get Naomi to safety."

Bill's eyes snapped. "I'm taking her *home*," he corrected. "Where she should have been this whole time. If she'd'a stayed home, none of this would'a happened." His sharp gaze drew down to her. "Ain't gonna make that mistake ever again."

Naomi's throat closed up, and she desperately drew in a breath. Her mind flailed – and latched onto her core.

Johnny and Polly.

Her voice rose high. "My children! Where are they? Are they all right?"

William gave her a reassuring smile. "They're fine, Naomi. We heard their hollering and found them at the edge of the woods. Elizabeth's with them. They're all right. We should go –"

Bill's voice gained an edge. "I done tole Elizabeth to take *my* children back to *my* house. She's there with them right now, if she knows what's good for her."

An icy steel entered William's voice, and he slowly turned to face Bill. "You threatened my wife?"

Bill's grin glittered in the firelight, and he flexed his free hand. He held William's gaze with a bright shine. "I done tole her a fact. Those are my children. They belong in my home – and nowhere else. She'll be waiting there with them, for when we get home."

His fingers tightened on Naomi's wrist. "So we best get going, woman. Back to your home, where you belong."

Naomi quickly nodded. She had to defuse the rising tension in the room. She had been around Bill's volatile temper for years, and she knew when he was walking the thin edge of an explosion. She would not let that unleash on the two men who meant so much to her.

"I'm ready to go," she agreed, stepping carefully across the blood-splattered floor, pulling Bill with her. "I need to get back to Polly and Johnny. They're probably scared out of their minds. I need to show them I'm all right."

Bill gave one last, dismissive look at the pile of bodies sprawled around the ramshackle room. His face lit up when his gaze landed on the bottle of whiskey the Carters had been sharing just minutes ago. He grabbed it with his free hand, his eyes glowing with satisfaction. Then he strode alongside Naomi out into the dark night.

He took the lead, hauling Naomi faster than she'd normally want, but she bit back any complaint and focused on keeping her feet under her. The snow was thick in drifts, and it caught at her feet, but Bill's strength dragged her through.

She could have been a deer carcass for all he seemed to care.

There were a pair of footsteps behind her, sure, steady, and she knew that David and William were keeping pace with them. The thought filled her with strength. For a while, at least, she was safe. She was being watched over.

Bill muttered and growled, groaned and spit, and they pushed their way through the brambles like a bull moose plowing his way to a mountain stream. Her face was raw with scratches and tiny whiplashes, but she didn't care. All that mattered was that she made it home to her two children.

Long minutes passed, filled with biting cold and shadowy dark. Tromping feet and frosty breath.

Finally they came over a ridge and her small shack was down beneath them, nestled into a clearing. It looked so tiny in the vast expanse of snow – a dollop of brown in a sea of white.

So fragile.

So alone.

Bill grunted in satisfaction, and then they were half-tumbling, half-sliding down the slope. They reached the door and Bill kicked it open, striding within.

Elizabeth was sitting on the floor by the fire, both children clinging tightly to her. At the noise, three pairs of eyes looked round. Then the children leapt to their feet. Johnny streaked toward his mother, and she bent down to swoop him up against her. Polly's crawl-toddle was slower, and Naomi moved to meet her, to draw her in the other arm.

Her resolve broke.

Naomi's sobs shook her, overwhelming her, and she hunkered down right where she was, wholly absorbed in her two young children.

Bill turned on the other three adults in the room. "Now, all a' ya, get out! You've made enough of a malahack."

Elizabeth drew to her feet. "But she's hurt! She needs –"

Bill raised a hand. "What she *needs*, woman, is to be left alone with her family."

William's eyes flared with heat, and he stepped forward –

Naomi shook herself, looking up at the people surrounding her. She forced her voice to hold steady. "I'm fine, really I am. Just a shock is all. I'm not hurt. You all go on home. Hiram needs you."

David glanced between Elizabeth and William. "You two go back and make sure Hiram's all right. I can stay and –"

Bill's hand clenched into a fist. "You gonna get out, is what you gonna do," he corrected. "You've done worn out your welcome." His

glower deepened. "You've already nearly gotten
Naomi turned into a whore. If they'd'a ruined her,
I'd a had to scourge her myself, to remove –"

David's eyes flashed.

Naomi pushed herself to her feet, both
children in her arms, and bit back the soul-deep
groan that threatened to billow out of her. Her
eyes met David's. "I'm fine. I need to wash up
and get some rest, is all. You go on home with
Elizabeth and William."

His amber eyes roiled with emotion. "You're
sure?"

She nodded, soaking in his strength. "I'm
sure. I'll be all right."

Elizabeth spoke up. "I'll come by tomorrow
and make sure you're all right. That you didn't
have any injuries that need tending to."

Bill growled. "My woman don't need no help
from outsiders."

Naomi glanced at him. "She don't mean no
harm, Bill. She's my sister, after all."

He gave a low humph. "We'll send for
someone if we need help. Which we won't. Now
get out. Naomi and I need to have a little talk."

Elizabeth's face creased in concern.

Naomi drew a smile onto her face. "I'm fine,
really, Elizabeth. Go home to Hiram."

Elizabeth looked like she might protest, but at
last she nodded. She held Naomi's gaze. "You get

some good food into you. Rest up. I'll check back in."

Naomi held her smile. "You all be careful on your way home."

Her eyes went to her brother. His gaze held tight concern, and she knew this was far from over. He would have an earful to say to her, once she was able to talk with him privately again.

She wondered if she'd ever have the chance.

Then her gaze moved to David.

He was bare from the waist up, his rippled muscles fitting neatly along his frame as if he'd been carved by God himself. She'd never seen a more handsome man in all her life. But it was his amber eyes which held her. Which comforted her, wrapped her, and made her whole.

Naomi's arms drew in Johnny and Polly against his shirt, against his safety, and for a long moment, she was protected. It was as if this token of his loyalty could keep them safe. She drew in a breath, surrounded by his musk, and her smile came from her soul.

David's eyes held hers, deep, and then he nodded.

The three adults quietly filed out of the house. The door closed, almost soundless, behind them.

Bill slowly turned, his eyes holding hers, a shine of anticipation coming into them.

"And now, woman, you and I are gonna have a little talk."

Chapter 10

Naomi moved quickly to the shelf, juggling her two children while she drew down the dented metal cup. She took the whiskey bottle from Bill and poured the cup as full as it would go, then placed it before the end chair. "You sit down, Bill, and rest a while. You done whooped the Carters good! They were mere haints by the time they crawled home. David and William barely had to blow at them a'fore they fell over, you'd beaten them so good. I bet you need some whiskey after that."

Bill seemed torn between wanting to bluster and to accept this enthusiastic praise – and he chose the latter. A sharp smile came to his face, and he nodded in acceptance as he strode to the chair and plunked down in it. He drew down a third of the cup in one, long swallow. "Damn right I did. Those boys didn't know what was coming."

"That's for sure," she agreed, putting the bottle within easy reach. "I'm gonna make you a special treat. We got that one piece of chicken left, and the three apples. I was waiting for New Year's for it, but I think you deserve it now. I'll have it ready in just ten minutes. You drink on up while I get that done."

He licked his lips. " 'Bout time we had some real food around here." He took another drink of his whiskey.

Naomi slipped into the bedroom, tucking Polly into her crib, then gently detangling Johnny from her neck. Her voice dropped to a whisper. "You two stay in here. Keep each other safe."

Johnny's large eyes held hers, and he mutely nodded.

She hurried back into the main room, gathered up her supplies, and started the soup. She used the last of the sage, the remnants of the salt, and even the few, precious bits of rosemary she'd been saving. She knew how close her tiny family was to destruction. Those bruises and cuts would put Bill in a gut-wrenching state, and anything was possible. She had to get him full – and to sleep. Get him at least through this first night.

And then in the morning she'd start over again.

As she stirred the soup, she glanced cautiously over at Bill. He seemed quieter than usual, staring at his whiskey cup, turning it slowly in place. It worried her. Was he planning something? He wasn't normally a man of deep thought. Usually he opted for sharp, direct action.

At last the soup was ready and she brought the bowl over to the pot. She ladled a large portion into the bowl, nearly filling it, and then carefully carried it over to place it in front of Bill. He took up the spoon and dove into it.

She quietly sat down at the table, watching him with cautious attention. "I'll catch us a mess of pumpkin seeds tomorrow. Get us well stocked. So we keep you at full health. And I can trade that summer dress of mine at the store for some more potatoes and apples. You're right – you should eat better."

He shook his head, slurping away at the soup. "Don't bother."

Tightness came to her throat. That wasn't like Bill at all. "What'd'ya mean?"

"Jerky'll travel easier, and we got the whole winter supply. Pack it up in a sack. You'll carry it just fine."

Naomi's blood ran cold. "Travel? Where are we going?"

His gaze was on his soup. "Been talking to the guys at the tavern about that there Luz-ana territory. Seems there's free land for the taking up north. In the mountains. Mount-ana. Hardly anyone up there. Too cold and isolated." A sharp grin came to his face. "Seems I'd like it just right."

Tension twined through Naomi. "You mean Missouri? The Missouri River?" That was hundreds of miles west. How could she see any of her family, with that kind of distance between them?

Bill's grin grew. "Nah, Naomi. I mean the far end of the Luz-ana Territory. 'Bout two thousand miles."

Naomi stared at him in stunned silence.

Two thousand miles.

Her head was shaking before she realized it. "But Bill – how am I supposed to see my family again? When the kids aren't babies any more, and we can go for visits –"

He gave a scoffing laugh. "Aren't babies? Woman, your job is to kick out babies. We're just getting the rust out of you. Now you'll start making 'em clean and proper, and I'll have a whole mess of 'em to put to work."

Naomi brought her hand protectively over her belly. "I don't understand."

Bill nudged his head back toward the bedroom. "You done wrong with those two. Came out dirty. Like an old pump, bringing up rusty water. But I seen it happen, when they put an Irish girl in with the negros to breed 'em. Sometimes

they come out dirty. Dumb. But then she get it
right and they come out proper."

His eyes drew to hers, pinning her in her chair.
"So you just best start making 'em proper. Else I
start selling off the ones we don't want. Can't feed
'em all. Need to be ready for when the good ones
come."

Naomi stared at him in disbelieving shock.
Surely he couldn't be saying what she thought he
was saying.

Her voice barely made it through her throat.
"But, Bill, they're *children*! They're innocent
children! It don't matter if their skin is black or
brown or tan. They're still the same on the
inside."

He gave a barking laugh. "Don't tell me you
believe that nonsense. What you see on the
outside is a sign of what's on the inside. Everyone
knows that. The darker the skin, the weaker the
man. Slower. Duller."

He drank down some of his whiskey. "A'least
the darkies can be trained. Pick the cotton and
such. Those Micks, they're too scrawny to be
much use. Weak, too. Why they're so cheap. Not
like a negro. Negro's a workhorse. Just need a
good whip behind him."

Naomi wrapped her arms around her. She had
always known Bill was this way – but she had

never seen the extreme he had gone to. She hadn't realized the depths to which his bias had sunk.

And now he would be raising their children.

Her mouth opened – and closed again. The thought of young Johnny and Polly growing up in this environment, hearing these words day-in and day-out, filled her with staggering despair.

She couldn't do it.

"I … I'll need to talk with my brother."

He shot her a steely look. "You won't be talking to no one at all," he warned her. "I'd a-hoped to wait for spring, but now's the time. We set out tomorrow." He took another scoop of his soup. "Good ta have food in a man before he sets out on a task."

Naomi stared again at the bedroom, at where her two tiny children huddled. Soon they would be walking through winter's worst cold, heading north, with no known destination. Every step would take her further away from her family.

She would be at Bill's mercy.

She found herself rising to her feet. The word eased out of her, a mere whisper. "No."

Bill glanced up. "What was that?"

She wrapped her arms around herself, around the shirt that David had provided to her. For her protection.

It was her armor.

Her voice grew in strength. "I can't do it. Not while Polly is so tiny. Not when it's frigid cold out there. Maybe in the springtime we can talk about it –"

His brow creased. "There won't be no talkin', and a'course we're goin'. You'll carry Polly, like ya always do, and that's final." He glanced around their tiny shack. "We sure as Hell aren't stayin' here."

Naomi blinked her eyes.

He was afraid.

For so long he'd seemed an insurmountable force, a torrential deluge without end, that it was hard to draw in the idea that he could fear anything else. But he had just stirred up a dirt dauber's nest with the Carters, and she had no doubt that they would be back in force.

Her voice was tremulous. "We could always go stay with my brother –"

Bill's eyes slowly rose.

Naomi realized, suddenly, that that was the worst possible thing she could have said.

He drew to his feet, the movement of a massive, riled bear preparing to charge. "Are you a-sayin' I'm *scared*?"

She put her hands up before her, backing up. "No! No! I was just thinking, with the injuries and all, that Elizabeth could –"

He swept at his chair, tossing it across the room. "I ain't scared a' no man. And I ain't gonna have no woman – no black squaw injun negro Mick – telling me where my family is a-gonna go!"

He stepped toward her, his body blotting out all light.

She spun in absolute panic, racing for the door, and yanked it open. She was half-way through when his hand grabbed hold of her long hair and yanked her back, flinging her hard on the wood floor.

Shooting pain seared through her abdomen. It swelled to engulf her soul.

She screamed.

The world went black.

Thank you for reading *Across the River.* The sequel, *In the Pines*, will be out shortly.

If you enjoyed this novel, please leave feedback on Amazon, Goodreads, and any other systems. Together we can help make a difference!
Be sure to sign up for my free newsletter! You'll get alerts of free books, discounts, and new releases. I run my own newsletter server – nobody else will ever see your email address. I promise!
http://www.lisashea.com/lisabase/subscribe.html

Please visit the following pages for news about free books, discounted releases, and new launches. Feel free to post questions there – I strive to answer within a day!
Facebook:
https://www.facebook.com/LisaSheaAuthor

Twitter:
https://twitter.com/LisaSheaAuthor

Google+:
https://plus.google.com/+LisaSheaAuthor/posts

Blog:
http://www.lisashea.com/lisabase/blog/

Share the news – we all want to enjoy interesting novels!

About the Story

I have wanted to write this story for a long, long time. Naomi Oxendine, born 1784, is a direct ancestor of mine. She endured a staggering amount of hardship in her life. I am extremely fortunate to have reams of records on her, because of a court case that her son, Johnny, was involved in. Much of the court case centered around race, perceptions of race, and interpretations of race. It is powerful, fascinating, depressing, and instructive, all at once.

Despite those records, there are still great swaths of information which has been lost over the years. Many records were destroyed during the Civil War. I take liberties with those "holes" to create a compelling story – but I strive to stay true to the known facts. My intention is to authentically present the many traumas that Naomi had to endure. To show my enduring respect for her tenacity and spirit in the face of great challenge.

The late 1700s and early 1800s were a tumultuous time in the American South. Irish slavery was just as horrific as African slavery, and yet it's rarely talked about. During those early years, there was often a sense of "we're all in this together" as colonists struggled to survive in a wild, new country. Blacks, whites, Portuguese, Lumbees, and others worked, fought, played, and loved. It was only as life became more "civilized" – and there was more to lose – that the whites in power took greater and greater steps to solidify the strata between them and the "others."

The topic of slavery, inter-race relations, and why people do what they do to other people is one that entire college degrees are based around. It would be impossible for me to encompass all the myriad of reasons and factors in short novellas. Still, I think the more we can be aware of what our ancestors went through, and where we came from, the better we can try to understand where we are now and make a path to a better future. For us, and for our next generation.

I am wholeheartedly proud to have Irish blood, Lumbee blood, African blood, and the many other streams which joined together to make me unique. I would hope that, someday, we can respect all people, of all colors, shapes, sizes, and backgrounds, and treasure them for their unique beauty and style.

In the end, we are all kin.

Naomi Oxendine

Naomi Oxendine, the historical one, was born in 1784 in Guilford County, North Carolina. She was the fifth of five children born to William Jackson. William had had the first child with one wife and then the remaining four with Margareth Liviston.

In the 1790 census Naomi was living with that family. Her father was still alive. He passed away in 1792.

Naomi's brother, William, married Elizabeth Oxendine sometime before 1800. There's no census for 1800 or 1810 because of the wars.

We know that in 1807 that Johnny was born, the child of Naomi and the "Devil" Bill Williams. In 1809 they had Polly. There's no record of Bill marrying Naomi.

That takes us as far as this first story ☺.

My lineage traces through Naomi's granddaughter, Elizabeth. This is a tintype that I own of Elizabeth. Like her grandmother she had long, straight, dark hair and mid-tone skin.

Glossary of Terms

Living in the 1800s in rural Tennessee meant absorbing a wealth of languages. There were Africans and Portuguese. Lumbee Indians and Irish. The flavors intermingled, and many of the words and terms can still be heard today.

A-gonna / a-fixin' / a-hopin': It was and is common in this area to add an "a" before –ing style verbs.

Across the River: poor, less worthy. The same meaning as "wrong side of the tracks" has now.

Chunked: tossed, threw

Crow: a derogatory word for blacks

Fixin' To: planning to

Gyp - female dog. A kinder term than the "B" one.

Haint – ghost. Now often pronounced as 'haunt'

In the pines - wealthy

Malahack – a mess

Meddlin' – interfering. Many of us now associate it with Scooby Doo and the "meddlin' kids" ☺

Pappy sack – playful nickname for a child

Pumpkin seed – a type of sunfish. Pumpkin seeds are easily-caught fish found all along the East Coast.

Sweetnins – a local word for sweets / desserts.

You See Me - do you understand?

Dedication

To the Boston Writer's Group, which supports me in all my writing quests. Ruth and Tom provided great encouragement and advice.

To Linda, Ruth, and Steve from my Oxendine genealogy group for their suggestions.

To my dad, George Waller, and to his mother, Jane Waller. Both of them adore genealogy and did immense amounts of research into the Oxendine family line. I owe much of my knowledge of this part of history to their efforts.

To David from my LinkedIn writing group, who writes in this genre and offered good advice.

Most of all, to my loyal fans who support me on Goodreads, Facebook, Twitter, and other platforms. It's because of you that I keep writing!

About the Author

Lisa Shea is the great, great, great, great, great granddaughter of the real Naomi Jackson. Both Lisa's father, George, and her grandmother, Jane, were avid genealogists and thoroughly researched this line of family history. Lisa owes an enormous debt of gratitude to both for their efforts.

Lisa has been dreaming about bringing this project to life for years, and is just so happy that it is now out for others to share.

All proceeds from the *Naomi Jackson* series benefits local battered women's shelters.

Lisa has written 41 fiction books, 81 non-fiction books, and 36 short stories.

Medieval romance novels:
Seeking the Truth
Knowing Yourself
A Sense of Duty
Creating Memories
Looking Back
Badge of Honor
Lady in Red
Finding Peace
Believing your Eyes
Trusting in Faith
Sworn Loyalty
In A Glance

Each medieval novel is a stand-alone story set in medieval England. The novels can be read in any order and have entirely separate casts of characters. In comparison, the below series are each linear and connected in nature.

Cozy murder mystery series:
Aspen Allegations | Birch Blackguards | Cedar Conundrums

Sci-fi adventure romance series:
Aquarian Awakenings | Betelgeuse Beguiling | Centauri Chaos | Draconis Discord

Dystopian journey series:
Into the Wasteland | He Who Was Living | Broken Images

Scottish regency time-travel series:
One Scottish Lass | A Time Apart | A Circle in Time

1800s Tennessee black / Native American series:
Across the River

Lisa's short stories:
Chartreuse | The Angst of Change | BAAC | Melting | Armsby

Black Cat short stories:
Lisa's 31-book cozy mini mystery series set in Salem Massachusetts begins with:
The Lucky Cat – Black Cat Vol. 1

Here are a few of Lisa's self-help books:

Secrets to Falling Asleep
Get Better Sleep to Improve Health and Reduce Stress

Dream Symbol Encyclopedia
Interpretation and Meaning of Dream Symbols

Lucid Dreaming Guide
Foster Creativity in a Lucid Dream State

Learning to say NO – and YES! To your Dream
Protect your goals while gently helping others succeed

Reduce Stress Instantly
Practical relaxation tips you can use right now for instant stress relief

Time Management Course
Learn to End Procrastination, Increase Productivity, and Reduce Stress

Simple Ways to Make the World Better for Everyone
Every day we wake up is a day to take a fresh path, to help a friend, and to improve our lives.

Author's proceeds from all these books benefit battered women's shelters.

"Be the change you wish to see in the world."

Made in the USA
Columbia, SC
15 April 2021

36142581R00071